This book belongs to

....

I celebrated World Book Day 2021
with this brilliant gift from my local
bookseller and Puffin Books.

#ShareAStory

WORLD BOOK DAY

World Book Day's mission is to offer every child and young person the opportunity to read and love books by giving you the chance to have a book of your own.

To find out more, and for loads of fun activities and recommendations to help you keep reading, visit **worldbookday.com**.

World Book Day is a charity funded by publishers and booksellers in the UK and Ireland.

World Book Day is also made possible by generous sponsorship from National Book Tokens and support from authors and illustrators.

LITTLE BADMAN

AND THE
RADIOACTIVE
SAMOSA

PUFFIN

PUFFIN BOOKS

UK | USA | Canada | Ireland | Australia
India | New Zealand | South Africa

Puffin Books is part of the Penguin Random House group of companies
whose addresses can be found at global.penguinrandomhouse.com.

www.penguin.co.uk   www.puffin.co.uk   www.ladybird.co.uk

First published 2021

001

Text copyright © Big Deal Films Ltd, 2021
Illustrations copyright © Aleksei Bitskoff, 2021

The moral right of the authors and illustrator has been asserted

Set in 13/18pt Bembo
Printed in Great Britain by Clays Ltd, Elcograf S.p.A.

The authorized representative in the EEA is Penguin Random House Ireland,
Morrison Chambers, 32 Nassau Street, Dublin D02 YH68

A CIP catalogue record for this book is available from the British Library

ISBN: 978–0–241–50925–8

All correspondence to:
Puffin Books
Penguin Random House Children's
One Embassy Gardens, 8 Viaduct Gardens
London SW11 7BW

HUMZA ARSHAD & HENRY WHITE

LITTLE BADMAN

AND THE RADIOACTIVE SAMOSA

Illustrated by
ALEKSEI BITSKOFF

PUFFIN

NEW TO LITTLE BADMAN?
MEET HUMZA AND HIS FRIENDS!

Humza
(AKA Little Badman)

This is me, Humza Khan – world-class rapper, legendary heart-throb and all-round hero. Yeah, I like to save the world now and then, but I don't let it go to my head. I'm probably the humblest person I know.

Umer

This is my best mate Umer. Is he a genius? Is he a bag of sand dressed as a boy? Honestly, I've no idea any more. He surprises me pretty regularly. But he's lovable, so I keep him around.

Wendy

Wendy actually *is* a genius. She's the smartest kid in our school by a mile. Hell, she knows more than all the teachers put together. She just needs a few lessons in how to misbehave. And I'm more than happy to help! ;-)

CHAPTER 1
DODGY DVD

Let me get straight to the point, yeah. I had ONE week of summer holidays left. One week to enjoy myself, hang out with friends and, most importantly of all, not have to save the world. Again!

I'm serious – there's been far too much world-saving going on this year for my liking. A kid needs his downtime. Aliens, evil geniuses, killer robots – this stuff's exhausting when you're twelve. All I wanted from my final week of holiday was to muck about around Eggington, get in trouble for annoying my neighbours, and maybe go swimming (if they ever got the pool fixed up, that is). Does that all sound like too much to ask? No, it doesn't!

But do you think that's how it went down? Yeah, right . . .

It all began when my best friend Umer rang my doorbell.

'Humza! Come quick!' he said, as I opened the front door to find his big excited face peering in at me.

'No way, man,' I told him. 'My dad just got a dodgy copy of the new Marvel movie off Market Abdul. I think someone used their phone to film it in a cinema or something, so you can't really make out what they're doing or saying, but who cares? We've got popcorn.' I lifted the bowl to show him.

'There isn't time for popcorn!' said Umer,

reaching in and helping himself to a handful. 'You need to see this right now!'

'Ah, man,' I said, shaking my head. 'Are you sure? Is it really life or death?'

'Humza,' replied Umer through a mouthful of popcorn, 'it's bigger than that.'

'Fine,' I said with a sigh, and I dropped my bowl on the hall table. 'Mum! I'm going out.'

'OK,' she replied from the living room. 'Be back before dark.'

'What about Captain Avengers movie?' shouted my dad. 'This cost me one pound seventy!'

'It's not my fault!' I yelled back. 'Umer's making me go.'

'Umer?' shouted my dad.

'Yes?' called Umer, leaning into the doorway.

'You want to stay and watch a film? Humza has to go out. You can have his popcorn.'

'Hey!' I yelled. 'Stop inviting my friends round to replace me.'

'Be a better son and I would not have to!' yelled my dad.

'Be a better dad and we could see films at the cinema!' I shouted back.

'WHY, YOU –' he bellowed, and I could hear him knocking things off the coffee table as he tried to stand up.

'Come on,' I told Umer. 'We'd better go before he figures out how to get off the sofa.'

Four minutes later we were standing in Umer's bedroom, looking down into a little cage.

'Aren't they amazing?' said Umer, beaming with pride.

'Um . . . I really hope you're not talking about these rats,' I replied, 'cos I could be eating popcorn and watching superheroes beating each other up right now.'

'They're not rats,' said Umer, looking offended. 'They're hamsters.'

They looked pretty ratty to me. They had ratty little faces, big ratty eyes, and they were crawling all over each other like . . . well . . . rats.

'This is what you dragged me round here for? To check out your plague rats?'

'They're *not* rats,' said Umer, rolling his eyes. 'My mum said I could either have hamsters or goldfish, so it was a no-brainer really.'

'I thought *all* your decisions were no-brainers?' I replied with a grin.

'Ha ha, very funny,' said Umer, without actually laughing. 'It doesn't really matter what you think. I *know* they're brilliant. I've been training them all day.'

'Training them?' I replied, raising an eyebrow. 'To do what? Poo and run round in circles? You can't train rats.'

'Hamsters!' snapped Umer. 'And yes you can. Watch this!'

He picked up a little silver whistle from beside the cage and gave it a small puff. The instant the shrill sound rang out, all six of the little rodents turned to look. They formed a line, standing up on their hind legs with their little arms held out, like they were begging.

'Good hamsters!' said Umer, picking up a pakora from beside the cage. He broke the little fried snack into pieces and gave each hamster an equal share.

'You feed them pakora?' I asked.

'They love it,' said Umer. 'They like bhaji and samosa too. But not daal. They won't touch it.'

'Huh, maybe they ain't so stupid after all,' I said, grinning. I'd rather eat week-old unwashed pants than a bowl of daal.

'Right, well,' I continued, 'as much as I've enjoyed your rat circus, I should probably be getting home.'

'What, already?' asked Umer, sounding disappointed.

'Umer, we've got less than a week before school starts,' I said, heading for the door. 'We have to fill this time with the most exciting, memorable and dangerous activities we can come up with. You whistling at rats *ain't* that.'

I opened the door and screamed:
'AARGHHHHH!'

Just inches from my nose, something with a great big face and bright yellow teeth was waiting to pounce!

CHAPTER 2

SHOWERS FORECAST

'Hello, Humza,' said Umer's mum.

She was peering in through the gap in the door, her face so close to mine I could smell the mango chutney on her breath.

'What you doing, man?' I shouted. 'You scared the hell out of me!' Then, for good measure, added, 'I mean, hi, nice to see you again.'

'You have a visitor, Umer,' she replied, with her usual friendly smile.

'Uh, yeah, obviously he does. I've been here for ten minutes,' I told her.

'No, not you,' she said, laughing. 'Extra visitor. Here to see mouse babies!'

'Hamster!' groaned Umer as his mum stepped aside to reveal Wendy Wang waiting behind her on the landing.

'Hi, guys,' said Wendy as Umer's mum waddled off to do whatever Umer's mum does when she ain't scaring me out of my skin.

'Oh, hey, Wendy,' I replied.

'Have you come to see my hamsters?' asked Umer, glowing with pride.

'I didn't know you had hamsters,' said Wendy. 'I just came to ask you about the meteor shower.'

'Huh?' I replied. 'What meteor shower?'

'Tomorrow,' said Wendy. 'Didn't you know?'

'We've been at camp all summer, remember?' I explained.

'Oh yes,' said Wendy. 'Of course you

have. Well, it's been on the news and in the papers. There's due to be a shower of meteors entering the Earth's atmosphere over the next twenty-four hours. Apparently it should be visible with the naked eye here in Eggington.'

'Whoa!' replied Umer. 'That sounds pretty cool.'

'Does it?' I asked. 'What's so good about a bunch of rocks falling out of the sky?'

'Well,' explained Wendy, 'for one thing, they'll be travelling so fast that they'll catch fire the moment they hit the atmosphere.'

'Really? How fast?' I replied.

'About one hundred and fifty thousand miles an hour,' said Wendy.

'Whoa!' I gasped. 'That *is* fast. My dad's car barely does thirty on a hill.'

'It should be pretty spectacular,' said Wendy, grinning. 'They call it nature's firework display.'

'Hmm . . . I like fireworks,' I said, slowly coming round to the idea.

'Great,' continued Wendy, 'because everyone's going up to the top of Muckweed Hill to watch after dark tomorrow night. You should come.'

'All right, then – count me in,' I replied. 'Just as long as I can convince my jailers to let me out after dark.'

Five minutes later I was headed home – not just because I wanted to ask my parents about the meteor shower, but because Umer had started his rat-whistling show again and I didn't think I could take it a second time round.

Turns out I don't much like rodents. I hadn't even realized until then. Now I could officially add them to the list of things I don't like, along with: daal, K-pop and the way my

Uncle Rabi's nose hair joins his moustache.

When I got home, though, I discovered I didn't need to worry about Mum and Dad letting me go to the meteor shower. I had something *much* worse to worry about than that . . .

'What do you mean you're coming too?' I cried.

'Of course we are coming!' shouted my dad. 'It is a once-in-a-life spectacular event! What, you think we are just going to sit at home and watch terrible-quality movie again?'

I glanced at the TV and the picture quality was even worse than before. Some guy in the cinema had sat down right in front of the camera and was blocking the whole screen.

'Fine,' I replied. 'But I'm hanging out with my friends. I don't want you embarrassing me all night long.'

'There will be a picnic,' said my mum with the smallest hint of a smile.

Damn. She had me there. Mum's picnics were the best.

'Will there be samosa?' I asked.

'Mm-hmm,' she said, nodding.

'Not for you, though!' said my father. 'They are all mine!'

'No way, man!' I yelled. 'Those are my favourite!'

'I thought gulab jamun were your favourite?' said Mum.

'Yeah, for dessert,' I replied. 'They're separate compartments, innit? Sweet and savoury.'

'Well, you'll be pleased to hear, we'll have gulab jamun too,' said my mum. 'So, will you be joining us, then?'

'Yeah, I guess so,' I replied. 'While there's food, at least.'

'Very kind of you,' said Mum with a grin.

Man, did that woman ever lose an argument? Never go up against a Pakistani mum. They're unbeatable. I swear, if Darth Vader had been a Pakistani mum, she'd still be running the Empire. But, you know, in a burka.

CHAPTER 3

EGGINGTONIANS

Wendy wasn't wrong. Everyone was there! It was like the whole town had turned out to watch the meteor shower. Muckweed Hill was swarming with Eggingtonians. That's what you call people from Eggington. Or at least that's what we call ourselves. The idiots in the next town over call us Eggheads. Whatever. Their town's called Marshfield, so we call them Marshmallows. Problem is, they call themselves Marshmallows too, so it ain't all that insulting when *we* say it. Stupid Marshmallows.

Anyway, everyone in Eggington was there, spread out across the whole of Muckweed Hill. There were picnic blankets and deckchairs scattered all over. Kids were running about with torches, screaming and playing. Grown-ups were talking and laughing. Uncles were telling stories and aunties were telling off uncles. It was a pretty amazing scene.

'There's a spot!' said Dad, hurrying right through someone's picnic to get to a patch of grass no bigger than a Twister mat.

'Hey!' shouted the man whose picnic Dad had just trampled. 'You stepped on my samosa!'

'Hey, yourself!' shouted my dad. 'Don't you know there's a meteor shower about to start! It is every man for himself!'

'Sorry,' said Mum as she passed the man. 'We have plenty of samosas to share.'

'No we don't!' I hissed at her as we made our way over to where Dad was spreading out our picnic blanket. 'Those are mine!'

'Actually, they're *mine*, Humza,' said my mum, in that voice that wasn't annoyed yet, but you knew it was hiding in there somewhere. 'You may have some if you're good.'

'Ah, man . . .' I groaned. 'When I'm rich, I'm gonna build my own samosa factory next to my mansion, so I can have samosas any

time of day or night.'

'That's nice, dear,' said Mum, who had clearly decided to stop listening.

As she and Dad began unpacking the food, I looked about for familiar faces. There was Jamal Jones and his family, digging into some jerk chicken that smelled amazing. And there was Iqbal Kota wrestling with his big brothers, who were busy hitting him with his own hands.

And then I spotted them: heading towards

me with big grins on their faces were Umer and Wendy. They were having to weave in and out through the crowd to avoid stepping on anyone. At one point, Umer lost his balance and nearly fell face first on a baby. The kid's mum didn't look pleased and started shouting at Umer. I could see him apologizing loads as he hurried away. He was still blushing when they arrived.

'Hey, Humza!' said Wendy. 'You made it!'

'Course I did,' I replied. 'Wouldn't have missed it. Where are you guys sitting?'

'I'm over there with my mum and dad,' said Umer, pointing to one side of the hill.

'My mum's on the other side,' said Wendy, pointing out her mum in the distance. Linda Wang was dancing by herself, holding a glow stick in each hand. She looked like she was having a good time.

'Aw, man, we're too spread out,' I said. 'I

wanna watch it with you guys, not with Old Man Ruin-Everything –' but as I nodded towards my dad, I let out a gasp. He had a mouth full of samosa!

'Hey!' I shouted. 'Don't eat all of those!'

'Why?' yelled Dad, firing crumbs everywhere. 'They belong to me!'

'Excuse me?' said my mum, looking stern.

'I just mean –' began my dad, realizing he'd said the wrong thing.

'Who cooked them?' continued my mum. 'Who purchased the ingredients? Who carried them up this hill?'

'I was only –' spluttered Dad, spitting out more bits of samosa. 'Look, I just –'

'They are MY samosas!' snapped my mum, reaching for the Tupperware box.

But somehow . . . it had vanished.

CHAPTER 4

HEAVY SHOWERS

By the time Mum noticed her samosas were missing, I was already running as fast as I could, clutching the box to my chest. Escaping ain't so easy when you're trying not to step on people's picnics and babies. Umer and Wendy were right behind me, doing their best to keep up.

'Humza!' yelled Umer. 'Did you just steal from your parents?'

'Nah,' I told him, pausing at the edge of the crowd. 'My mum wants me to eat well. She'll remember that in a day or two, once she's stopped being angry. And by then there'll be no samosas left, so no point arguing.'

And they were fine-looking samosas. There must have been twenty of them. Golden brown, crispy triangles of delicious deep-fried goodness.

'Oooh! Samosas!' came an excited voice beside me, as a hand reached in and grabbed one.

'Hey! Those are mine!' I shouted, turning to see who'd had the nerve to steal my stolen samosas.

Oh no! Auntie Uzma! She could chomp down twenty samosas without stopping for breath! I had to get out of there – and fast!

'Hello, Humza,' said my uncle, who was sitting beside her on their picnic blanket, near the edge of the crowd. His name's Tariq but everyone just calls him Grandpa, cos he looks older than the Earth.

'*Mmmmm!*' said Auntie Uzma, munching down on the stolen samosa. 'Your mother's – I can tell! They are my favourite.'

'Mine too!' I shouted, yanking the box away as she reached for another.

'Run, Humza!' hissed Grandpa, leaning towards me. 'Run while you still have some left!' He flashed me a big grin, and I grinned back at him, before turning and sprinting off into the dark, with Umer and Wendy following close behind. There was only one way we were going to be able to watch this meteor storm safely, and that was by ourselves!

We found a spot a few hundred metres away, far enough from the crowd that we could only just hear the shouts and cheers as everyone waited for the meteor shower to begin. It was pitch black – perfect for looking up at the stars.

'This'll do,' I said, dropping to my knees and popping the box of samosas down between us.

'What are we doing all the way out here?' asked Umer, who was still panting a bit from our run.

'I had to protect these samosas, didn't I?' I told him. 'They're the best thing ever. And as you two were part of the heist, you can each have one.' I held out the box and they both helped themselves to a samosa.

Just as Wendy was about to take a bite of hers, she gasped. 'Look!' she cried, pointing.

We all turned just in time to see a bright point of light slice through the night sky above us. It looked exactly like a star – just as small and just as bright – but it was moving fast. Super fast!

'Whoa!' I gasped.

'Awesome!' murmured Umer.

'I've only ever seen them in movies,' said Wendy, captivated, the light reflecting in her glasses. 'It's so much better in person.'

'Will there be more?' asked Umer once the meteor had faded into darkness.

'Of course,' said Wendy. 'That's why they call it a shower. There should be lots.'

And she wasn't wrong. A moment later there came another. Then another. Then more than I could count! They were beautiful, lighting up a little slice of the darkness then vanishing as quickly as they'd appeared. Wendy was right – it *was* a natural firework display!

'Hey, Wendy,' I said a moment later, as we lay there in the grass, watching the sky. 'You don't reckon one of them could hit us, do you?'

'Hit us?' replied Wendy, turning to look at me.

'Yeah . . . I mean, they're directly above us, aren't they?' I explained. 'What if one of 'em smacked Umer in the head? He'd be killed.'

'Why does it have to be *me*?' asked Umer, frowning.

'Don't worry,' said Wendy confidently. 'They burn up in the atmosphere. That's what creates the bright lights we're seeing. They're just little bits of rock, and as they approach the Earth, they get super hot, catch fire and disintegrate. They're much too small to make it all the way to the ground.'

'Oh, that's good,' I replied.

And then my samosas exploded.

CHAPTER 5

BANG

It was like a firework going off in my face. There was a boom and a flash of light as my poor, sweet samosas were blasted into the air.

'Aargh!' I screamed, diving for cover.

'Look out!' yelled Wendy, pulling Umer to one side.

We heard a series of dull thuds as samosas began to rain down all over us. When it felt safe to look again, I opened my eyes. The Tupperware box was lying on its side, smoking. It was completely empty!

'Oh, man!' I cried. 'My samosas!'

'*What* was that?' groaned Umer, looking up.

'I've no idea,' said Wendy, who was still half covering Umer, having dragged him to safety.

'Hey, look at that,' I said to Wendy. 'You saved Umer.'

'Oh yeah,' said Umer, grinning. 'Thanks.'

'Um, that's OK,' said Wendy, getting up.

'Hey! Why didn't you save me?' I asked, suddenly feeling a bit offended.

'Um . . . Umer was closer,' replied Wendy, who might or might not have been blushing

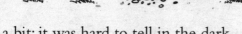

a bit; it was hard to tell in the dark.

'I thought you said those things wouldn't hit us, Wendy,' I muttered, getting to my feet.

'They can't have,' she replied. 'It's impossible.'

'Obviously not,' I said, shaking my head. 'It totally took out my samosa.'

'Not totally,' said Umer. 'Look.'

He pointed down to where a nearby samosa lay in the grass. Even though it was totally dark where we were, I could still see it. It was almost as though the samosa was glowing slightly. But that was ridiculous. Whoever heard of a glowing samosa?

'Amazing!' I said, and grabbed it. 'At least there's one left!'

'Hey, there's another,' said Wendy, pointing to another illuminated triangle glowing in the darkness.

'Oh yeah,' I said, scooping up the Tupperware box and hurrying over to the next samosa.

'And another,' said Umer, picking one up from beside him.

'They're everywhere,' said Wendy. 'I don't think they're even broken. Your mum makes a tough samosa, Humza.'

'You should see her roti,' I replied. 'After two days sitting out, it's harder than steel. I swear, you can cut diamonds with a shard of my mum's roti.'

'Here you go,' said Umer, dumping five samosas into my box. Wendy added three more. And after another minute or so, we'd found them all.

Once the samosas were all piled together in the box, it was impossible to ignore the glow that was coming off them.

'I can't believe we got hit by a meteor and

survived,' I said. 'If that had been a direct hit, we'd have been goners.'

'Looks like the shower's stopped now,' said Wendy. 'We should be safe.'

'Come on, let's get back to the others,' added Umer. 'I don't want my parents to leave without me.'

'Fine, but let's walk slowly,' I replied, reaching for a samosa. 'I want to enjoy at least one of these before my dad gets his hands on them again.'

I took a bite of the delicious snack, my teeth crunching through the crispy pastry and into the curried vegetables inside. *Ah, man . . .!* That was good.

'G'you wamp wum?' I asked the others.

They must have understood, because they reached in and took a samosa each.

'Actually, you know what?' I said once I'd swallowed. 'These are too good to risk my dad getting his hands on them. Can you look after them for me, Umer?'

'Sure,' he replied, accepting the box. 'I'll keep them safe.'

As we walked back up the hill, none of us said another word. We were too busy enjoying the best glowing samosas in the galaxy . . .

CHAPTER 6
BAD DREAM

Have you ever had one of those weird dreams that seem to last the entire night? I swear, my head was spinning from the moment it hit the pillow. I kept dreaming about comets hurtling through space, me hanging off the back, spinning and weaving past massive flying samosas. It was pretty bizarre. When I eventually woke up, I felt like I'd been on a journey halfway round the solar system. My bed was all damp with sweat, and I'd kicked my blankets and pillows on to the floor.

I was just getting my clothes on when I heard the phone ring in the hall.

'HUMZA!' shouted my dad a moment later. 'Umer is on the telephone! Tell him not to call so early! I have not even had my third cup of chai!'

'Stop shouting!' I yelled as I marched downstairs and snatched the phone out of his hand.

'Don't you pull that face at me!' said my dad when he saw me.

'What you talking about?' I replied. 'I ain't pulling no face!'

'Really? Because you look ridiculous!' he muttered, wrinkling up his nose. 'It's like you slept face down on a pile of bricks!'

'Go away. This is private,' I snapped, turning my back on him.

'Nothing is private in my house!' shouted Dad. 'Until you are eighteen, every thought you have belongs to me!'

'GO AWAY!' I yelled.

'My house, my rules!' grumbled Dad as he walked back into the living room.

'What's up, man?' I said to Umer eventually.

'Um . . . are you . . . *OK*?' he asked, sounding a bit weird.

'Yeah, I'm fine,' I replied. 'Why?'

'Are you sure?' he continued.

'I think so . . . Why? Aren't you?'

For a moment there was no reply.

'I need to show you something,' he said.

'Ah, man, not those stupid rats again! I've already seen 'em, remember? I was deeply unimpressed.'

'No, something else. Something super serious.'

'You better not be messing with me this time. You're worse than that kid who cried wolf – what's his name?'

'The boy who cried wolf?' suggested Umer.

'Yeah, that's him.'

'I'm not messing with you, Humza. I swear. Something weird's happening. I need to show you. Meet me in the secret spot. Ten minutes. I'll tell Wendy.'

'Fine,' I said. 'I'll head out now.'

'Humza,' he added, 'are you sure you're all right?'

'Yes!' I snapped, turning to look at myself in the hallway mirror. 'Obviously I'm fi–'

That was as far as I got. Turns out I wasn't fine. I wasn't fine at all. Something was badly wrong. My beautiful, perfect, adorable face! What had happened to it?

It was all smushed up to one side, like it was made out of silly putty! Dad was right – I did look like I'd slept face down on a pile of bricks. And, for some reason, everything had stayed like that – all squashed up and ugly!

'Aargh!' I yelled, dropping the phone.

'Humza?' came Umer's tinny voice from the dangling handset. 'Humza? Are you OK?'

But I wasn't OK . . . I was a monster!

CHAPTER 7

SUPER WEIRD

I ran to the bathroom, turned on the tap, and splashed water all over my face. When I looked back in the mirror, I was prepared for the worst. But, blinking away the water, I could see immediately that everything was back to normal. My face just looked like . . . *me*.

'Oh, thank God,' I gasped. I'd never been so pleased to see me in all my life. Had I been dreaming? Was the whole thing just in my head? It was the weirdest thing that had happened to me in . . . well, in a couple of weeks at least. I do lead a pretty strange life, I guess.

Anyway, I decided everything was probably fine after all and that I must have imagined it. So now I just had to find out what the heck was up with Umer. He sounded like he'd really got himself worked up about something.

Ten minutes later I was in the park, heading for our 'secret spot'. It was a place no one else knew about, right in the middle of some massive bushes.

You know the kind of bushes you can cut into shapes, like people or animals or whatever? Well, in Eggington, some imaginative gardener had chosen a great big rectangle. From a distance, it looked just like this huge block of green, all angular and neatly pruned. But we'd discovered that, if you got on your hands and knees, with your belly in the dirt, you could shuffle between the bushes and crawl into the centre. Once you were inside, it opened out and there was a space about the size of a big lift or small Pizza Hut – you know, the kind that only does takeaway.

The little clearing was surrounded on all sides by big, bushy walls. There was no ceiling though, so you could look up and see the sky. And once you were in, no one outside in the park could see you. It was like being right in the middle of the world's simplest hedge maze.

I was shuffling through the gap on my elbows and knees when I spotted Umer in there, already waiting for me.

'Hey, man,' I said, 'what's all the fuss about?'

'Hey, Hum–' he began, but his mouth fell open before he could finish. His eyes bulged like a pair of overinflated beach balls.

'What's the matter?' I asked as I went to stand up.

But, for some reason, I couldn't get to my feet. I was stuck there, resting on my elbows. I turned and looked back to see what I was caught on. The sight made me yell out loud . . .

'AARGHHH!' I cried. 'What's wrong with MY BUM?!?!'

Somehow, I'd left my backside stuck in the hedge! I'd managed to crawl away from it, stretching my waist out like it was made of chewing gum! I must have been seven feet tall now. I could see that my trousers were caught on a low branch, which was stopping me from climbing through.

'Humza!' Umer gasped. 'You're stretchy!'

'What the hell?' I cried. 'Why's my bum over there?'

'*Humza?*' came another voice, from outside of the bush. It was Wendy. '*Move-so-I-can-get-in,*' she said. Her voice sounded weird. Much quicker than usual, like she was racing to get each word out. As she spoke, I could feel her prodding me on the bottom.

'Aargh!' I yelled. 'Stop prodding my bum! I'm stuck!'

'*Hold-on,*' said Wendy, and, with that, she gave me a massive shove.

The little branch I was caught on snapped

at once and my lower half came flying into the clearing. My bum slammed into me, sending me crashing towards Umer. Just as I was about to roll into him, he squawked, leapt into the air – and vanished.

Suddenly, where Umer had been, there was now a plump white chicken. The panicked bird was flapping its wings and doing its best to fly.

'Umer?' I said to the chicken as it lost control and crashed head first into the ground.

'**Bwark!**' said Umer the chicken, looking up at me from between my legs.

That's when I realized my lower half was back to normal again. Wendy's shove had pushed my body back into its usual shape. I was Humza-height again!

Just then, Wendy's face appeared in the leafy gap.

'Wendy!' I yelled. 'Umer's a chicken!'

'*I-can-see-that,*' said Wendy, talking so fast I could barely understand her. '*There-he-is, right-there-in-front-of-me, but-he-looks-like-a-chicken-and-not-like-a-boy! Remarkable!*'

'Whoa! Whoa!' I cried. 'Slow down! I can't understand you!'

'*I-can't-slow-down!*' babbled Wendy. '*I-want-to, but-my-brain's-racing-at-a-million-miles-an-hour!*'

'Just breathe,' said the chicken in Umer's voice.

'You can talk!' I gasped, turning to the Umer-chicken.

'I guess so,' he replied, and, the moment he said it, there was a loud *POP!* and Umer turned back into Umer.

He was crouching in the dirt, holding his arms out like chicken wings and looking very panicked and confused.

'What's going on?' he yelled.

'I don't know, man!' I cried. 'I just left my bum in a bush, you turned into a chicken, and Wendy's talking at the speed of light! What's happened to us?'

There was a moment's pause, before all three of us shouted at once –

'THE SAMOSAS!'

CHAPTER 8
PLAYTIME

'So let me get this straight,' said Umer once all three of us had sat down inside our bush to work things out. 'That meteorite did something to the samosas. We ate the samosas. And now we have . . . *powers*?'

'Right,' I replied. 'If you can call them that. They seem pretty useless to me. I'm stretchier than old underwear elastic, Wendy's brain's in overdrive, and you turn into random stuff whenever you get spooked. We're like the worst X-Men ever.'

'*Well-maybe-we-just-need-some-practice?*' said

Wendy, sounding like one of the chipmunks from that cartoon.

'Slow!' I told her. 'Take it slow!'

Wendy stopped and breathed.

'*Well . . .*' she began, pausing between each word, '*maybe . . . we . . . just . . . need . . . some . . . practice . . .?*'

'There, much better,' I replied.

'But what do you mean, "practice"?' added Umer. 'I didn't choose to turn into a chicken.'

Wendy breathed again, then continued at an only slightly speedy rate: '*My brain is racing at a million miles an hour,*' she explained. '*But if I concentrate, I can control it. I can speak normally.*'

'That's still pretty fast, actually,' I told her.

'*Fine, almost normally then,*' she replied. '*But perhaps we all just need some time to practise. To find out what we're capable of.*'

'Hmm . . . That ain't gonna be easy inside this bush,' I said, looking about the cramped space. 'What if Umer turns into an elephant? We'll all be crushed.'

'And we can't use the park,' added Umer. 'It's much too crowded. What if someone sees us? My parents will be furious if they find out I turned into a chicken.'

'*We need to go somewhere where there aren't any people,*' said Wendy. '*Where there's plenty of room, and where it doesn't matter if we break stuff.*'

'I know just the place!' I shouted, jumping up. 'Follow me!'

Quarter of an hour later, we stood in the junkyard right at the edge of town. It was the last bit of Eggington that separated us from those idiots in Marshfield. My mum had made me promise not to play there in case an old fridge fell on me or I got trapped under a landslide of car tyres. But that was before I had superpowers. I figured it was probably fine now.

It was a great spot. There was junk everywhere! Big piles of electronic appliances. Huge stacks of mashed-up cars. And about a billion bags and boxes of who knows what. There were big open sections where we'd have enough space to test out our powers, and these were all connected together by dirty old roads, just wide enough for a truck to drive down. It was perfect.

'*All right, who wants to go first?*' asked Wendy, still a bit fast but easy enough to understand.

'Um . . . how?' replied Umer.

'*Just concentrate,*' she told him. '*Try to focus on what you want to turn into. Anything you like.*'

Umer clenched his fists, screwed up his face and strained as hard as he could. Nothing happened.

'Well, unless you're trying to turn into a badly dressed Asian kid, it ain't working,' I said.

'Shut up,' snapped Umer. 'My mum says I look dapper.'

'*I know how to resolve this,*' said Wendy in her super-fast way. '*Umer simply requires the right stimulus.*'

And, with that, she threw a tin can at his head.

'Aaarrgh!' Umer shouted, and immediately turned into a tortoise. The tin can whistled over him as his little head disappeared into its shell.

Umer the tortoise poked his face out and looked around. When he realized he was safe, he suddenly turned back into normal Umer with a ***pop!***

'Amazing!' I cried. 'Well done, Wendy! Now use that giant brain of yours to figure out how to make my stretchiness useful.'

'*Well,*' buzzed Wendy, '*I've been thinking about that. How far can you reach?*'

'What do you mean?' I asked.

'*Try picking something up, like that football over there.*'

Wendy pointed to an old deflated football ten metres away.

'OK,' I said, and I began to walk towards the football.

'*No,*' said Wendy. '*Keep your feet exactly where they are. Just reach.*'

'Um . . . all right,' I said, and I reached out towards the ball.

Whooooosshhh! My hands rocketed away from me! In an instant, my arms were ten metres long! I grabbed hold of the ball.

'Whoa!' I gasped. 'Awesome!'

'*Now bring it back,*' said Wendy.

I concentrated and tugged my hands towards me. They suddenly whipped back in my direction, like when you release the lock on a tape measure. In a flash, the ball was in my hands.

'*Now throw it at Umer,*' said Wendy with a grin.

'Hey, wait!' shouted Umer as the ball whizzed towards him.

Pop! Suddenly Umer was a bowl of nachos. The ball whizzed over the top of him and landed in a nearby pile of junk.

'Ha!' I laughed. 'Umer! You're nachos! Mind if I have one?'

With another *pop!*, Umer turned back into himself.

'Don't eat me!' he yelled. 'And stop throwing things at my head! It's weird turning into stuff when you don't want to.'

'*I think you should be able to control it,*' said Wendy. '*Just like Humza can. You just need to remember what it feels like when you're about to change, then try to reproduce that feeling.*'

'Um . . . OK,' replied Umer, who didn't look like he really understood.

'What about you, Wendy?' I said. 'I mean, it's pretty cool that you can figure all this out with your mega-brain, but that can't be *all* you can do, can it?'

'*I'm happy just being smart,*' she said with a smile.

'Uh-huh. Or maybe Umer's not the only

one who needs the right motivation,' I said with a grin, then hurled a tomato at her.

The rotting piece of fruit spun through the air towards Wendy's head. It was just about to smash into her face when it froze. It hung there, as if by magic. Wendy seemed to be concentrating on it very hard. She'd almost gone cross-eyed.

'Whoa!' I gasped. 'How'd you do that?'

'*Hmm*,' said Wendy, considering what had just happened. '*It seems you were correct. I just needed the right stimulus to access the full potential of my powers. I appear to be able to control matter with my mind.*'

'This is awesome,' said Umer. 'We're basically superheroes!'

'Not yet, we're not,' I replied. 'We're still missing something.'

'*Really? What's that?*' asked Wendy.

'Costumes!'

CHAPTER 9
SECRET IDENTITIES

What better place to find crazy stuff to make superhero costumes than a junkyard! The way I figured it, superheroes needed secret identities, and that meant disguises. That's just how it's done.

After fifteen minutes of rooting through rubbish and trying things on, we all met back in the middle of the junkyard to show off our alter egos.

'Whoa! You guys look brilliant!' I said when I saw them.

Wendy was wearing an old silver-coloured

ski suit she'd found, and she'd made a purple mask and matching belt with some sequinned material torn from the world's ugliest blouse.

Umer was dressed in an orange jumpsuit, a bit like the kind of thing prisoners wear. He'd put his bright red pants on over the top, to give himself that authentic superhero look, and had made a matching mask out of a bit of ripped-up curtain.

Me, I'd pulled my hat down over my eyes and cut two holes in it so I could see. I'd found a black T-shirt for some old rock band with a big red 'R' on the front, along with a matching red belt (which was probably made for women but worked pretty well for superheroes too). For my cape, I'd tied a shiny black bedsheet round my neck, which looked pretty sweet blowing behind me in the breeze. Most importantly of all, though, I had found myself a shield.

'Humza,' said Umer, staring quizzically at the shield in my hand, 'is that . . . *roti*?'

'Not just roti,' I replied. '*Week-old* roti! The hardest substance known to man!'

You see, I'd discovered a rubbish bag full of waste from a curry restaurant. Inside was a stack of old rotis – just as unbreakable as my mum's! I don't know if you've ever tried to eat week-old roti, but it'd be easier to eat a manhole cover. So, by giving it a handle, I'd turned it into a rock-hard shield – just like Captain America's! But, you know, a bit more Pakistani, innit!

'So what's your superhero name, then?' asked Umer.

'Well, I considered Badman, obviously,' I explained. 'But it was just a little bit too close to Batman.'

'That's true,' said Umer. 'Plus everyone round here already knows you call yourself Little Badman. It's hardly a secret identity.'

'Exactly,' I agreed. 'That's why I went with something even better. You can call me . . . *Roti-man!*'

And, with that, I whipped my shield hand out, launching my roti as far away from me as I could without ever letting go of it. My arm stretched thinner and thinner as my shield flew through the air and eventually crashed right through the window of an old

Ford Fiesta twenty metres away. As the glass exploded everywhere, I tugged my hand back towards myself, shield and all. An instant later, my roti was right back in front of me, not even scratched. I held it up and grinned.

'Pretty sweet, huh?' I said.

'Awesome!' cried Umer. 'And, from now on, you can call me *Pakora Boy*!'

As he said it, Umer clenched his face tight, concentrating as hard as he could. All of a sudden he turned into a giant piece of pakora. Stood up on its end like that, it must have been five metres tall. For a moment, it wobbled back and forth, then it toppled over, crushing a fridge freezer that was standing nearby. With a *pop!*, Umer was Umer again.

'*You're getting good at that,*' said Wendy. '*But why Pakora Boy?*'

'It's my favourite snack,' replied Umer, grinning. 'Plus, when I could only find orange stuff to wear, I figured I kinda looked a bit like pakora. So it was the obvious choice really.'

'How about you, Wendy?' I asked. 'What's your superhero name?'

'*Me?*' said Wendy, before striking a classic superhero pose. '*The name's Calculation . . . Miss Calculation!*'

'OK then, Miss Calculation,' said Umer. 'Your turn to break something!'

'*Really?*' said Wendy, giggling. '*OK then!*'

She held out one hand, concentrating as hard as she could, then lifted a washing machine high into the air with only the power of her massive brain!

'Whoooaaaa!' gasped Umer.

With a flick of her wrist, Wendy sent the washing machine flying through the air. It landed with a **BOOM!** somewhere out of sight – and, before any of us could say another word, there came a yell from over in the same direction.

'Hey!' cried the voice. 'Stop throwing things at us!'

'*Whoops,*' whispered Wendy, looking worried. '*I hope I didn't hit anyone!*'

'It sounded like a kid,' I said. 'What are they doing here? A junkyard's no place for children!'

'Should we hide?' asked Umer.

'Why?' I replied. 'We're already in disguise. And anyway, we're superheroes! What's there to be afraid of?'

But no sooner had I said it, than a powerful whirlwind began to rise up around us, hemming us in. Dust and rubbish from all around lifted off the ground, spinning into a cyclone ten metres across. We were surrounded by it on all sides! Trapped!

Nothing to be afraid of? I definitely spoke too soon . . .

CHAPTER 10
MARSHMALLOWS!

'What's happening?' shouted Umer over the roar of the swirling tornado.

Before I could reply, I felt a tug on my shield and it was yanked out of my hand.

'Hey!' I yelled. The rock-hard roti began to dance away from me as though it had come to life. 'What the hell is this?'

Wendy, whose gigantic brain was already working on an answer, reached down and grabbed a handful of dust from her feet. She hurled it in the direction of my retreating roti shield, where it crashed into something invisible! A dusty smear, roughly the shape of a person, was suddenly revealed, floating in the air beside us.

The mysterious smudge began to cough and splutter. Almost immediately, it turned into a girl. She was dressed in a bright blue tracksuit, along with what looked like a slightly battered Halloween cat mask.

'Croaker!' she yelled. 'Catch!'

And, with that, she threw the shield upward, right over the dust tornado that was still blocking us in. I stretched my arms out to grab it, but – just before I could reach the roti – something pink and slimy whipped out of nowhere, wrapped itself round the shield and yanked it from the sky.

I watched as the roti shot through the air, right into the hands of a boy. He was wearing a large pair of fishing waders, a tattered green surfer's wetsuit and a set of yellow-tinted goggles – the kind welders use. Weirdest of all, though, was his mouth. From out of his lips stretched an enormous pink tongue! It was still wrapped firmly round my shield. With a loud slurp, the boy whipped his horrible tongue back into his mouth, before leaping into the air . . . TEN METRES into the air!

He crashed down beside the girl in the cat mask, smirking and holding my shield up like a trophy. It was at that instant that the cause of the whirlwind became clear. Another boy, this one wearing a bright yellow onesie and a yellow motorcycle helmet, skidded to a stop beside his friends. He'd been running round us this whole time – so fast that we couldn't even see him! *He* had created the circular wall of dust!

'What are you doing in our junkyard?' growled the boy in yellow.

'*Your* junkyard?' I snarled back at him. 'This

is *our* junkyard. If you're not from Eggington, you can't use it!'

'I should have guessed,' sneered the boy. 'Eggheads!'

Umer gasped. '*Marshmallows!*'

'That's right,' said the girl in the cat mask. 'And this junkyard is part of Marshfield. It separates our town from you rotten Eggheads!'

'No, it doesn't!' I shouted. 'It's part of Eggington and it separates us from you stupid Marshmallows!'

'Liar!' shouted the frog-looking boy in the goggles.

'Trespassers!' shouted Umer.

'*Stop it!*' said Wendy, whose planet-sized brain obviously had no time for bickering. '*None of this matters. What matters is that you have superpowers like us. How's that possible?*'

'None of your business!' said the girl, before adding, 'How come *you've* got superpowers?'

'None of *your* business!' snapped Umer.

'You probably haven't got very good powers,' said the boy in the yellow onesie. 'Not like me, Yellow Streak!'

'Or me, Invisi-cat!' added the girl.

'Or me, Croaker!' jeered the boy with the frog-like tongue.

There was a moment's pause before Umer and I burst out laughing.

'Shut up!' said Yellow Streak. 'Stop laughing at us! They're good names!'

But we couldn't help ourselves. These guys were ridiculous!

'What are *your* names, then?' demanded Invisi-cat.

'*I* . . .' said Wendy, stepping forward, '*am Miss Calculation!*'

'And I'm Pakora Boy!' added Umer, striking the most dynamic pose a guy in an orange jumpsuit can strike.

'And you can call me . . . Roti-man!' I declared.

Once again, a moment's silence passed before laughter filled the air. This time, though, it was us three feeling foolish while those idiot Marshmallows fell about in hysterics.

'Roti-man?' said Croaker, bent over double, howling.

'Pakora Boy?' sneered Invisi-cat, throwing her head back with laughter.

'And why would you call yourself *Miscalculation?*' said Yellow Streak. 'Doesn't that mean *mistake?*'

'It's two separate words: Miss and Calculation! It's a pun,' growled Wendy. *'And, anyway, you can't talk! Yellow Streak means cowardly!'*

'Does it?' replied the boy, his laughter stopping at once. 'Oh . . . I thought it sounded familiar. Still, doesn't matter. The point is, you're not welcome here! This is our junkyard. So clear off!'

'What are you talking about?' I asked, laughing. 'You're the ones who aren't welcome. Go back to Marshfield!'

'We're in Marshfield! *You* go back to Eggington!' yelled Invisi-cat.

'This *is* Eggington!' shouted Umer.

'No it's not,' yelled Croaker. 'This is Marshfield! *You're* the ones trespassing!'

'There's only one way to settle this,' I said, taking a step towards Yellow Streak.

'Superhero fight?' he suggested.

'Superhero fight,' I replied.

Things in the junkyard were about to get messy . . .

CHAPTER 11
POWER HUNGRY

Umer was the first to act. There was a sudden *pop!* and he vanished. In his place was an enormous chicken. It must have been seven metres tall!

'A chicken, Umer?' I yelled. 'Seriously?'

'Bwark!' squawked the chicken, before adding (in Umer's voice), 'I panicked.'

I saw Yellow Streak take a few steps back in surprise. Then he began to laugh.

'*That's* your power?' he said, shaking his head. 'This is going to be easier than I thought!'

And that's when the first egg hit him, drenching him in yolk. It was huge! Easily as big as a watermelon. It nearly knocked him off his feet. There was yolk everywhere! I turned round to see what had happened.

Wendy was already using her mega-brain to pick up another egg from near Umer's feet.

'*Keep 'em coming, Umer!*' shouted Wendy, as she fired the egg towards Invisi-cat.

The girl only had a moment to turn invisible before the giant egg crashed into her, exploding everywhere. Invisi-cat couldn't hide now – she was dripping in yolk!

'Good work, guys!' I yelled. 'Now to get my shield back . . .'

There was a flash of movement above me as something green shot through the air. It was Croaker, mid jump! I dived out of the way, just in time to avoid being hit by his disgusting tongue. I fired my fists out towards him, my arms stretching thin. As he whistled overhead, I caught hold of my shield and tugged it back to earth. Croaker, who'd been caught off guard by my stretchiness, was sent spinning. He crashed head first into an enormous pile of used nappies.

I whipped my shield back towards me, just in time to see a yellow flash out of the corner of my eye – but I was too late to stop it. Suddenly, I was tumbling over backwards, tripped up by something I never saw coming. Man, that guy was too fast!

I went to throw my arms and legs out, hoping to catch hold of one of his feet and knock him off balance. But, instead of stretching out like usual, nothing happened. I just lay there on the ground, flapping my limbs about like I was making a snow angel.

At that same moment, Umer turned back into normal old Umer, and the egg Wendy was lifting with her mind fell from the sky and splattered in the dirt.

'Something's wrong! I can't feel my powers,' said Wendy, and for the first time that morning her voice sounded back to normal.

And it looked like it wasn't just us three having superpower problems. Yellow Streak was moving at a normal speed now, and Invisi-cat was standing there beside him, as clear as day. Croaker was still trying to jump into the air, but now he couldn't manage to get much higher than a foot off the ground. He stopped hopping about after a moment and stuck out his tongue. It looked just like yours or mine, short and pink and stubby.

'Our powers!' said Umer. 'They're gone!'

'I had wondered if this might happen,' said Wendy. 'It looks like the effects are only temporary.'

'You mean we've lost our powers for good?' I asked.

'Not necessarily,' replied Wendy. 'But, if we want to experience them again, we'll need to consume more samosas.'

'So, if *we* want to stay this way,' asked Yellow Streak, who'd been listening in, 'we'll need to eat more chicken nuggets?'

'*Chicken nuggets?*' I replied.

'That's right,' he answered. 'Something hit

our bargain bucket of nuggets during the meteor shower. We just dusted them off and ate them anyway. Didn't really think about it until we woke up with superpowers.'

'All right, then,' said Umer, nodding. 'You go home and get more nuggets; we'll go back to mine and get another round of samosas. Then we'll meet you back here to settle this thing!'

'Agreed,' said Croaker.

And, with that, the Marshmallows turned and hurried away, back towards the Marshfield gate.

'Shall we change back into our normal clothes?' asked Wendy as we hurried towards our own gate.

'No time,' I replied. 'We need to get to Umer's and top up. Fast.'

I couldn't wait to become stretchy again, especially as it meant having another delicious samosa. But I was about to discover that Umer's house wasn't any safer than mine. Turns out my dad wasn't the only one who couldn't be trusted around samosas . . .

CHAPTER 12
ROAAAARRRRRRRRR!

As soon as we ran into Umer's bedroom, we saw it. The lid of the Tupperware box was lying on the carpet. Every single one of the samosas had VANISHED!

'I don't understand!' cried Umer. 'I left them right here.'

'If your mum's eaten a dozen space-samosas,' I replied, 'we're gonna have a seriously angry supervillain on our hands.'

'No way – she wouldn't have,' said Umer, shaking his head. 'I told my parents they were yours. They wouldn't have touched them.'

'Um, guys,' said Wendy. 'I think I know what might have happened.'

She was facing the other way, looking at the desk, where the hamster cage stood. The *empty* hamster cage!

'Oh no!' Umer gasped. 'They've escaped!'

'And they've eaten all my samosas!' I cried.

'Are you sure it was them?' replied Umer, clearly not wanting to believe it.

'Have you got a *better* theory?' I snapped. 'The cage is wide open, the samosas are missing, and all that's left in the box is a bunch of tiny brown poos! I don't think we need CSI to solve this one, do you?'

'What do you suppose happens when hamsters eat space-samosas?' asked Wendy.

No one said a word. I don't think we wanted to consider it. But something told me we weren't going to have a choice. Umer had left his bedroom window open. Wherever the hamsters were now, they weren't in here . . .

Out in the garden, we all began hunting around – in bushes, under plant pots, behind the shed . . . anywhere we could think of that a hamster might hide.

'Maybe they're invisible, like that cat girl,' suggested Umer.

'Or maybe they've turned into chickens like you and flown away?' I replied.

'Chickens can't really fly,' replied Wendy.

'OK, penguins then. You know what I mean.'

'Maybe we're worrying over nothing,' said Umer, who was crouching near the garden table. 'Maybe it only works on people. They're probably just normal hamsters still. Nothing to be concerned about.'

And that's when we heard it . . .

'ROAAAAAAARRRRRR!'

It came from nearby, maybe next door – it was hard to say. It sounded like a lion but . . . bigger.

'Wh-wh-wh-what was that?' stammered Umer.

'Probably nothing,' I replied.

'Really?' he said, looking puzzled.

'No, you idiot! It's obviously a giant radioactive hamster! What do you think it was?'

Something was moving on the other side of the fence. I could hear plants snapping beneath heavy footsteps.

I could hear breathing . . .

Grunting . . .

And then . . . silence.

None of us breathed. None of us moved an inch. Eventually Umer looked up at me.

'Do you think it's gone?' he whispered.

And that's when the whole fence exploded.

'*ROAAAAAARRRRRR!*'

An elephant-sized hamster burst through the wall, sending wooden shards flying in every direction.

'*AARRRRGGGHHHHH!*'

we all screamed.

This thing was a monster! It must have been five metres tall. It had huge, dripping fangs, muscles like The Rock, and the angriest eyes I'd seen since I 'accidentally' flushed my dad's car keys down the toilet.

'RUN!' I shouted.

'This way!' said Umer, pointing to a gap between the two houses.

The alley was big enough for the three of us to escape down, but there was no way a monster like that was fitting through. We moved so fast we'd have given Yellow Streak a run for his money. The big, nasty beast was foaming at the mouth, gnashing its fangs. It charged after us, but we were too quick.

I was the last one into the alley and I could hear it right behind me. There was a huge **CRASH!** as it slammed into the wall of Umer's house. Just as we'd hoped, it was too

massive to make it through. I could hear it biting and snapping behind me.

'**Go! Go! Go!**' I shouted, and we ran without looking back.

I don't know how long we ran for, but when we eventually came to a stop, no one could speak. We were all panting hard. My heart was pounding such a crazy beat you could have freestyled to it.

'We have to do something,' said Wendy when she could speak again. 'What if they hurt someone?'

'What can we do against those things?' I cried. 'We ain't got no superpowers!'

'Maybe not,' replied Wendy, 'but we know who does . . .'

Umer and I stared at her.

'You have got to be kidding!' I said, shaking my head. 'Those guys? We can't ask a bunch of Marshmallows for help!'

'But they're the only ones with any meteorite snacks left,' said Wendy.

'Maybe they'll share them with us?' suggested Umer.

'Are you mad?' I yelled. 'They hate us! They already hated us before you threw giant eggs at them! Our towns are arch-enemies going back thousands of years – maybe millions! What makes you think they'd help us now?'

'Because,' said Umer, 'they called themselves superheroes. Superheroes do what's right, even when they don't want to.'

He had a point. I didn't want to ask the Marshmallows for help, but I had to admit it, it wasn't just my choice any more. Roti-man had a say in things now, and I knew what he'd choose.

'Fine,' I said. 'We'll ask. But I doubt they'll help us. They're Marshmallows after all.'

CHAPTER 13

IF YOU CAN'T BEAT 'EM . . .

We raced back into the junkyard, where the Marshmallows were already waiting for us.

'Ah, there you are!' said Yellow Streak, making a fist with one hand and punching the palm of the other. 'Ready to fight again?'

'Fight's off,' I said, skidding to a halt. 'We need to work together.'

'What are you talking about?' said Invisicat, looking suspicious.

'Giant hamsters!' shouted Umer, still panting. 'They ate our samosas! Now they're on the loose!'

'We need to stop them,' added Wendy. 'Will you share your chicken nuggets with us so we can all fight them together?'

The three Marshmallow superheroes looked at each other for a moment, looked back at us, then burst out laughing.

'That's the worst attempt at a lie I've ever heard!' said Yellow Streak. 'You really think we'd give up our last three nuggets over rubbish like that?'

'We're not lying!' I yelled. 'It's true. And if you don't believe us, we'll just have to prove it to you.' I turned to Umer. 'Do it,' I told him.

Umer nodded, then slipped the little silver whistle from his pocket. The Marshmallows didn't say a word as they watched him take an enormous breath. He placed the whistle between his lips. And then he blew – as hard and as long as he could. The whistle let out an ear-piercing screech.

'Hey! Stop that!' cried Croaker. 'That's really annoying!'

'Get ready,' warned Umer, looking around.

At first, there was nothing. Everything was silent. Then I began to hear it, a distant rumbling. I could feel the ground beneath my feet beginning to shake.

'What's going on?' said Yellow Streak, starting to look a little nervous.

The sound was clearly coming from the direction of the Eggington gate. Closer and closer every second.

'Time to run,' said Wendy.

'Yup,' I replied, and the three of us began to run towards the Marshfield exit. The

Marshfield superheroes stood their ground, though, waiting to see what the noise might be.

They didn't have to wait long. I glanced back just in time to see a wall of garbage explode in every direction. There, standing in the centre of the pile of destroyed rubbish, was an enormous, snarling five-metre-tall hamster.

Umer, Wendy and I weren't gonna stick around to watch what happened next – not without our superpowers. The last thing I saw, before we fled round the corner, was Invisi-cat vanishing into thin air, just as Croaker leapt high into the sky, narrowly avoiding the creature's gnashing teeth.

Suddenly, there was a blur of movement as Yellow Streak appeared at my side. He slowed down to keep pace with us as we charged towards the exit.

'You weren't lying!' he yelled.

'No!' I shouted. 'And there are five more of those things out there. So are you gonna help us round 'em up or not?'

'You made *SIX* of them?' Yellow Streak cried.

'Not on purpose!' I yelled back.

And the moment I said it, we came face to face with two more of the monsters. They were blocking the Marshfield exit and stomping right towards us.

'Uh-oh!' said Umer. 'We're trapped!'

'Here,' said Yellow Streak, pulling a sandwich bag from his pocket.

Inside were three glowing chicken nuggets.

'They're all that's left,' he added. 'Take one each, while I distract those things.'

'Thanks, man,' I said, reaching for the bag. 'You're a lifesaver!'

I held the nuggets out to Umer and

Wendy, who took one each. The moment we all had one, Yellow Streak sprinted off towards the giant hamsters, disappearing in a flash of gold. He was brave, you had to give him that.

I was just about to take a bite of my glowing nugget when I froze.

'Hey, Yellow Streak,' I shouted, 'are these halal?'

When he heard me, Yellow Streak skidded to a stop and looked back over his shoulder.

'Halal?' he replied. 'I've no idea. Why?'

'Where'd you get 'em from?' I shouted.

Suddenly something crashed to the ground beside me. It was Croaker.

'You'd better run!' he shouted, pointing behind us.

I glanced back, just in time to see two more hamsters bounding down the path in our direction.

'*AARRRGGGHHHH!*'

screamed everyone. Clutching my uneaten nugget, I ran towards the gate. Yellow Streak had managed to distract the two hamsters that were blocking our path, sprinting in circles round them until they were dizzy and confused. He'd given us a chance!

We all made a mad dash for the exit. But the dizzy hamsters weren't down yet. They began stumbling towards us, gnashing their teeth. Umer and I dodged one way, Wendy and Croaker dived the other. In the panic, we got split up. The two dizzy creatures were now right between us, and another pair were in hot pursuit! There was no time to stop and sort out the halal question – my nugget would have to wait. We needed to get out of there before they cut us off!

CHAPTER 14
ROOSTER BURGER

Umer and I made our move, sprinting past one of the two hamsters Yellow Streak had been distracting. It gnashed its teeth at us as we came close, but we were too quick, and it was too dizzy.

'Why couldn't you have just gone for goldfish?' I shouted at Umer as we hurried towards the exit.

'I didn't know they'd turn into monsters!' yelled Umer.

'You mean these are *your* hamsters?' came a voice beside us.

All of a sudden, Invisi-cat appeared next to me, running as fast as she could.

'Whoa! Where'd you come from?' I yelled, as we dashed through the gate and into the street.

'Follow me!' she shouted as we sprinted into the quiet road behind the dump. 'We need to get out of here before those things tear us apart! Have you got your powers back yet?'

'Not yet,' I yelled. 'Do you know where those nuggets came from?'

'Uh . . . yeah – Rooster Burger,' she replied, panting for breath as we tore down the road.

'Great,' I said, turning to Umer. 'Quick, man, give me your phone!'

'Here,' he replied, pulling his rubbish old mobile out of his pants.

I didn't have time to be disgusted.

'Operator! Put me through to Rooster

Burger in Marshfield!' I shouted when the woman at directory enquiries answered.

'*One moment, sir,*' she replied.

I glanced back just in time to see not one, but *three* huge hamsters crash out of the big gates and into the street behind us. I hoped Wendy was all right in there. I figured she must have eaten her nugget by now. She didn't have to worry about her food being halal like me and Umer did. It's a Muslim thing, to do with how the meat's prepared. But even without her powers, I figured Wendy was still the smartest of us by a mile. I knew she'd be all right. Or at least I prayed she would be . . .

'Down here!' hissed Invisi-cat, pointing to an alleyway.

Before the hamsters could spot us, Umer and I followed her into the narrow lane that led off the street between two buildings.

Halfway down, we ducked behind a great big wheelie bin, just as the phone at Rooster Burger picked up.

'*Hello, Rooster Burger,*' came a teenager's voice.

'Hey, I need to know if your chicken nuggets are halal,' I hissed.

'*Um . . . what?*' he replied, sounding confused.

'Halal!' I snapped, a bit louder. 'You do know what halal is, don't you?'

'Humza! Quiet!' whispered Umer, nodding towards the end of the alley.

I stole a quick peek and realized that one of the giant hamsters was sniffing around right where the alleyway led off the street. The moment Invisi-cat saw it, she vanished beside me. Umer and I were suddenly alone.

'*Um . . . the thing is . . .*' came the voice down the phone, '*I've only worked here for, like, two days, so . . . uh . . .*'

'Well, is there someone you can ask?' I growled.

'*Uh . . . hold on,*' he replied. '*Steve? Are our nuggets "hamal"?*'

'Halal!' I snapped.

'*Uh . . . "halal",*' he repeated.

There was a moment's pause. I could picture Steve thinking about it, scratching his oily forehead. At the end of the alley, there was a crunching sound as the enormous hamster began making its way towards us.

'*Hello?*' came the voice on the phone once again.

'Yes, I'm still here,' I whispered.

'*I spoke to my manager, Steve, and he says all our nuggets are definitely halal.*'

'Tell Steve I love him,' I said and hung up, immediately stuffing the nugget into my mouth.

CHAPTER 15

DRIVE TIME

'How long do we have to wait?' whispered Umer, swallowing down the rest of his nugget and slipping his phone back into his pants.

'Shouldn't be long this time,' replied Invisi-cat, reappearing out of nowhere. 'Mine took a few minutes.'

'I thought you'd left?' I said.

'No, I just went to find a way out,' she replied. 'We need to get to the other end of the alley. Your friend's down there waiting for us.'

'Wendy?' I gasped, before quickly adding,

'Uh . . . I mean, Miss Calculation.'

'Yeah, she's with Tim . . . uh, I mean, Yellow Streak,' replied Invisi-cat.

'But how will we get there?' asked Umer. 'That monster's right behind us.'

'Don't worry – I've got this,' said Invisi-cat, before vanishing. Beside us, a glass bottle suddenly lifted off the ground and began floating up the alley, towards the mutant hamster. Umer and I peered out to watch, doing our best not to be seen.

The bottle had drifted to within just a few metres of the hamster before the creature noticed it there, hovering in the air. The enormous beast began to snarl, white foam dripping from its fangs. It looked like it was just about to pounce, when suddenly the bottle hurled itself through the air, right over the hamster's head. The creature turned and charged after it, like a dog fetching a stick. The bottle smashed down in the distance, shattering to pieces, just as Invisi-cat reappeared beside us.

'Run!' she yelled.

The three of us turned and ran towards the other end of the alley as fast as we could manage. As we tore out into the street, I spotted Wendy. She was sitting in the driver's seat of a totally wrecked car. At first I thought it was a convertible until I realized that it was just seriously torn up. The roof was missing, the doors were ripped off, the bonnet was smashed in. It must have come from the dump. There was no way this car was going anywhere.

'*Jump in! Quick!*' shouted Wendy.

'Are you crazy!' I replied, running over to her. 'This car ain't gonna move!'

'*Humza,*' replied Wendy, '*there's no time to discuss it. My nugget's already kicked in and my* brain's in overdrive again! You're just going to have to trust me!'

'I can work with that,' said Umer, jumping into the back of the car.

Invisi-cat looked at me, I looked at Wendy, then glanced down the street. All six hamsters were charging towards us from the far end! If we didn't move, they'd be on top of us in fifteen seconds.

'This had better work,' I shouted, leaping in beside Wendy.

Invisi-cat climbed into the back next to Umer and put her seat belt on. It seemed like a good idea, so I did the same. There was a sudden thump as Croaker crashed down on the other side of Umer. We had a full ride.

'*Everybody in?*' said Wendy, glancing round.

'What about Yellow Streak?' I asked.

Wendy grinned.

'*Yellow Streak,*' she shouted, '*hit it!*'

I glanced over my shoulder to see Yellow Streak waiting behind the car. Over his shoulder I could see the hamsters, now less than ten metres away. We only had a few seconds before they'd be on top of us!

But Yellow Streak didn't look worried. The moment he placed his hands on the rear bumper, we took off!

WHHHOOOSSSSHHHH!!!

Oh! My! God! I'd never felt acceleration like it!

With Yellow Streak as our engine, we exploded out of there like a rocket ship. The hamsters disappeared behind us in a flash as we hurtled down the street. With no roof and no windows, the wind in my face was like a fire hose blasting me into the seat.

We whipped round a corner, barely slowing down. Wendy was steering, work-ing the handbrake, manoeuvring us round obstacles like an F1 driver. That brain of hers was letting her drive better than any ordinary person could ever hope to – especially a kid who'd never had a driving lesson in her life! It was incredible!

At least, it was until the handbrake snapped off . . .

'Uh-oh,' said Wendy, looking at the broken metal rod in her hand.

We were going at a hundred miles an hour, with no brakes, and heading for what looked like a solid brick wall. 'Uh-oh' didn't really cover it . . .

CHAPTER 16
BRACE YOURSELVES

Yellow Streak may have been great at making us go fast, but it didn't look like he had a plan for slowing us down. I saw him do his best to bring us to a halt by grabbing hold of the rear bumper. But, as he tugged it, it just came off in his hands. He crashed to the ground, tumbling over and over until he came to a stop. But *we* just kept going.

'It's been nice knowing you, guys,' I said, looking from Wendy to Umer.

But Umer wasn't there. In his place was a tortoise. He'd pulled his head into his shell again and was trembling like Scooby-Doo when he sees a ghost.

And then it hit me! If Umer's powers were back then so were mine! There was still time!

'*What are you doing?*' shouted Wendy as I ripped off my seat belt and jumped up.

I threw my hands out in front of me, feeling my arms stretch longer and longer as I reached towards the bonnet. I grabbed hold of the underside of the car, making sure I had a strong grip.

'Hold my feet!' I shouted as I stepped into the back seat. 'TIGHT!'

Croaker and Invisi-cat grabbed one shoe each and held on with all their might. Once they had me, I lifted my head up high, until the wind caught my body, pulling me out of the car – all of me except my hands and feet, that is, which still held fast to the vehicle. Every other inch of me ballooned to full stretch. I was suddenly spread out in the sky, catching the air like a huge parachute!

I held on with everything I had. In the back seat, Croaker and Invisi-cat were doing the same – hanging on to one shoe each. Straight away the car began to slow. The wall was still rushing towards us, but the harder we strained, the more we began to decelerate.

'Brace yourselves!' I shouted. We were still going too fast for my parachute to stop us.

An instant later, the car slammed into the wall. Everyone still had their seat belts on, thankfully, or they'd have all been thrown out of the vehicle. Instead, only *I* went flying.

Luckily, though, it turns out stretchy guys bounce. I crashed into the wall, before rebounding straight back off it like silly

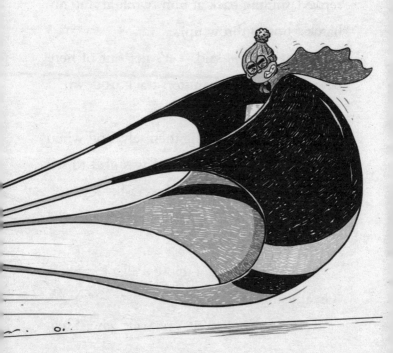

putty. I ended up wrapped round a lamp post half a block away, my head spinning.

'That was amazing!' came a voice beneath me a moment later.

I looked down to see Yellow Streak standing in the street.

'I couldn't have done it without you,' I replied, smiling back at him (while trying my hardest not to throw up).

'Come on,' he said. 'Let's get out of here before those killer hamsters track us down.'

The others were dusting themselves off when we arrived back at the car. I was glad to see no one had been hurt in the crash.

'Are you OK?' asked Umer when he spotted us.

'Yeah. That was a close call,' I replied. 'Great teamwork, though.'

Everyone looked at everyone else. Then

we all burst out laughing. I guessed these guys weren't so bad after all.

'We need to stop those things,' said Invisi-cat, once the laughter had finished.

'But how?' replied Croaker. 'They're too strong.'

'*Well,*' said Wendy, thinking it through with that mega-brain of hers. '*We do know that these powers don't last forever. Which means, if we can trap them somewhere, we should just be able to wait out the clock.*'

'OK, but where do you trap six massive hamsters?' asked Umer.

And suddenly I knew! I had the answer! The very thing I'd been moaning about for months was about to save our lives!

'I've got it!' I yelled.

'*Really? What?*' asked Wendy.

'Get your trunks,' I said with a grin. 'We're going to the swimming pool!'

CHAPTER 17

GOOD PLAN,
ROTI-MAN

Fifteen minutes later we were standing inside the Eggington swimming baths, looking over the edge of the main pool. It had been completely drained of water and stripped of tiles for months now, and it still looked far from being finished. The pool was nothing more than a big hole in the ground.

'That'll never be deep enough,' said Umer, his voice echoing around us. 'A killer hamster could climb out of there without breaking a sweat.'

'Do hamsters sweat?' asked Croaker.

'I've no idea,' replied Umer, shrugging.

'How is that important right now?' I snapped. 'Anyway, this ain't the pool I meant. Follow me.'

I led them towards the big doors at the far end of the room.

'*Of course!*' said Wendy, realizing what I was getting at. '*The diving pool!*'

Back in the nineties, Eggington had been home to a champion diver. It was only for about a second, but the town had decided it'd be a good idea to spend all its money putting in a proper diving pool. There was a regulation-sized Olympic diving board, which must have been ten metres high, and the pool itself was easily that deep again, maybe deeper. Like the main pool, it had been drained for repair. It was perfect.

'That's gotta be deep enough,' I said,

looking into the pit. 'There's no way one of those things could climb out of there.'

'It's a good plan, Roti-man,' said Yellow Streak. 'This might actually work.'

'I sure hope so,' I replied. 'You all know what you've got to do?'

Everyone nodded. They all looked super

serious. If I'd had a camera with me, I'd have grabbed a shot. It would have totally been the picture for the DVD cover. I swear, one of these days I'm gonna get a smart phone so I can start photographing this stuff. I'm sick of no one believing me! My Instagram would be bigger than Beyoncé's if I posted half of what I've seen this year. Dinosaurs, aliens, killer robots – that's much more interesting than Jay-Z in his pants!

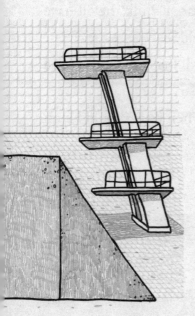

'All right, Umer,' I said, 'time to call those hamsters.'

'OK, then,' he replied, looking a bit nervous. 'Here goes nothing . . .'

He took a deep breath. Put his whistle to his lips. And blew . . .

SHRRREEEEEEEEEEPPP!

Standing in the big, empty swimming baths, the whistle was louder than ever. We all covered our ears until it was over. Umer was red in the face by the time he'd finished.

'Wow,' said Invisi-cat. 'I think they'll have heard that in Marshfield.'

'They'll have heard that in China,' said Croaker, rubbing his ears.

'Good,' I replied. 'Then they should be on their way . . .'

CHAPTER 18
RODENT RUMBLE

We heard them before we saw them. The rumbling. You could feel it in your chest. All six of us stood lined up round the edge of the diving pool. From there, we looked out across the whole length of the complex, over the main pool to where the big doors at the end led out to the reception area.

We'd made sure to leave the main doors to the street wide open, but I was worried that even that wouldn't be a big enough gap for a mutant hamster to fit through. The

next sound we heard confirmed that I'd
been right –

KER-RUNNNCHHHHH!!!

It was the noise of the front entrance being
bulldozed as something big charged into the
building.

'Get ready,' I told the others and, as I said
it, the doors to the main pool exploded open.

'ROAAAAARRRRRRRR!'

bellowed the hamster as it burst into the
room. The moment it spotted us, it charged.

Behind it, a second and then a third
hamster smashed its way in. They leapt into
the main pool and straight back out the
other side, no hint of trouble. They were still
coming for us. I just hoped that the diving
pool would be deep enough to trap them.

The first hamster crashed through the
doorway between the main pool and the

diving pool, demolishing the brickwork on either side. It was time to teach these rodents a lesson.

'Hey, rat face!' I shouted, running towards the snarling monster. 'Come get me!'

The hamster charged in my direction, right towards the edge of the deep pool. At the very last second, just as I could feel its hot breath upon me, I whipped out my hands, arms stretching thin, and grabbed hold of the diving board high above me. I pulled myself out of there just as the monster's fangs gnashed at my feet, missing by millimetres.

The massive creature tried to slow itself, but it was no good. It was far too big and travelling far too quickly. It tumbled over the edge and into the empty diving pool below. It crashed down in a cloud of dust and broken tiles, roaring with anger. It was trapped!

'Hey, you!' shouted Yellow Streak, heading

off the next hamster to arrive in the room. 'Here I am! Take your best shot!'

The beast snarled at him and charged. Yellow Streak left it to the last possible moment before, in a flash, sprinting to safety. The heavy monster followed its friend head first into the pool with a cry. Yellow Streak skidded to a stop at the far side of the room, just as the third hamster burst in through the broken doorway.

At that same instant, the wall behind Yellow Streak exploded, showering him in bricks and plaster. One of the other hamsters had clearly decided to make its own entrance. Rather than coming through the main doors, it had simply ripped a wall down, catching Yellow Streak off guard and burying him in debris.

Now we were cornered! And with no sign of Yellow Streak beneath the rubble, it looked like he was out of action! This wasn't going as well as I'd hoped . . .

And then I noticed Wendy. She had her fingers held to her temples and was concentrating hard. Just as the wall-smashing hamster began to stomp into the room, the bricks at its feet began to rise into the air. There beneath them was Yellow Streak. He was unhurt, lying on the floor inside a protective bubble. Wendy was using her superpower to create a force field! She'd prevented Yellow Streak from being crushed!

'Wendy, you did it!' I shouted.

But she was concentrating too hard to answer. She lifted her hand out towards the snarling hamster and, as she did so, the hovering bricks began to fly towards the beast. It leapt back in surprise as half a ton of debris rained down on its head.

Wendy pushed her other hand through

the air, as though shoving something away. An invisible force connected with the great monster's side, knocking it towards the edge of the pool. The hamster lost its footing and tumbled in, crashing down on its siblings.

'Three down, three to go!' cheered Croaker, just as the next hamster was almost on him. 'And this one's mine!'

CHAPTER 19
HAMSTER HOLE

Before the hamster could sink its teeth into him, Croaker jumped high into the air, flipping twice and landing effortlessly on the creature's massive head. He whipped out his tongue, spun it around like a lasso, then slapped it down, wrapping it round the hamster's eyes, over and over again, until the confused monster couldn't see a thing. It roared in anger, trying desperately to claw Croaker from its head.

But Croaker was too quick, dodging left and right to avoid the blows, his enormous tongue never loosening its hold over the hamster's eyes. The furious creature spun and twisted, until it was so dizzy it could barely stand up.

At the very last moment, just before the beast tumbled over the edge, Croaker leapt from its back and landed beside me. The monstrous rodent fell into the pool, crashing down on to the other three.

'Here come the last two!' shouted Invisi-cat, charging forward.

One hamster had appeared through the hole leading out to the street and the other through the shattered doorway to the main pool. Just as the first creature dived towards her, Invisi-cat vanished. The confused hamster tried unsuccessfully to slow itself down, before losing its balance and tumbling head over paws into the diving pool.

But the other one hadn't been fooled. It

had just enough time to skid to a halt at the edge of the pit. Its head spun round, its nose twitching. It could still smell Invisi-cat!

Suddenly the monster lunged.

'Aaarghhhh!' screamed Invisi-cat.

She reappeared instantly, gripped in the claws of the monstrous beast! It opened its enormous mouth, revealing razor-sharp teeth! I couldn't watch!

And then, just in that last moment, before the hamster could take a bite out of Invisi-cat, something crashed into its back, knocking Invisi-cat to safety.

We all turned to look. It was *another* giant hamster! Were there seven of these things now?

'Stay away from my friend!' said the huge bright orange hamster that had just saved Invisi-cat.

'Umer?' I cried. 'Is that you?'

'Yup,' replied the orange hamster, 'but you can call me Pakora Boy!'

The furious mutant hamster charged towards Umer, foaming at the mouth. But Umer was ready for it. He caught the monster by its paws and, using its own weight against it, spun it towards the edge of the pool.

The hamster let out a shriek as it lost its footing and tumbled towards the pit. But in that last instant, it reached out one stubby claw and grabbed hold of Umer's leg, tugging him in after it!

'NOOOOOO!' I cried as the orange hamster lost his balance and fell into the snarling mass of murderous rodents.

CHAPTER 20
BWAAARRRRRKKKK!

In an instant, Umer was gone. All I could
see down there was a swirling mess of hair
and claws and fangs. The mutant hamsters
were enraged at having been trapped, and
now poor Umer was stuck in there with
them.

'*Where is he?*' cried Wendy, peering over
the edge.

'I can't see him!' I shouted.

Had they eaten him already? This was
terrible! This was worse than terrible! No
boy should be eaten by his own pet hamsters.

'*Wait! What's that?*' said Wendy, pointing.

Suddenly, there was the strangest sound.

'BWAAAARRRKKKKK!'

cried a chicken, launching up from the middle of the hamster pit. The panicked bird rocketed skywards, away from the mouths of the ravenous monsters. Umer was flapping his wings like crazy, propelling himself as high as he could with his useless chicken wings. The hamsters were snarling and gnashing, climbing over one another to get to him.

'Another chicken! Seriously?' I shouted. 'Of all the birds in the world, why another chicken?'

But now wasn't the time to call Umer an idiot. At any second he'd start falling back down. I threw out one hand, reaching above me to grab for the far end of the diving board. With the other, I lunged towards my best friend the chicken. I felt my feet leave the ground as I swung over the pit like Tarzan.

With my free hand stretched out in front of me, I grabbed for Umer, just managing to catch hold of him before he tumbled back down. The monsters below us howled in fury as we sailed over their heads, crashing to the ground on the other side of the pool. Almost immediately, Umer turned back into Umer.

'That was too close,' he said, shaking his head.

'Never, ever, ever do something that stupid again!' I shouted.

'What?' asked Umer, looking puzzled. 'You mean risk my life to save the day?'

'No!' I yelled. 'I mean turn into a chicken when you need to fly to safety! What were you thinking?'

Umer stared at me wide-eyed for a moment. Then a grin began to spread across his face. Mine too. Soon, everyone was laughing. Well, everyone except those big ugly monsters in the pit. They kept raging and snapping and shrieking for ages.

And then, all of a sudden, they stopped.

The battle had been over for about twenty minutes, and we'd spent the time sitting in the rubble, laughing about it and reliving the best bits.

'Hey, listen,' said Wendy once the snarling from below had disappeared. 'They've gone quiet.'

'Oh yeah,' I replied. 'And you're not speaking fast any more.'

'You're right! I hadn't even noticed,' said Wendy. 'My mind's stopped racing.'

I stretched out a hand as far as I could.

Normal length. My stretchiness was gone.

All six of us walked to the edge of the pool and looked down. There, at the bottom of the pit, were six very small, perfectly happy hamsters.

'They're OK!' cried Umer, a huge grin exploding across his face.

I think it was the happiest I'd ever seen him.

Once we'd fished Umer's rodents out of the pool, using a super-long net we found in a cupboard, we made our way back out into the street. We were still dressed in our superhero costumes, which, to be honest, had begun to feel kinda silly since we didn't have our superpowers any more.

I was the first to take my mask off, rolling it back into a normal hat. The others quickly followed. Soon, all six of us were standing there in the sunshine, grinning at one another. It was the first time we'd seen each other's faces properly. Turns out Yellow Streak, Invisi-cat and Croaker were also known as Tim, Maya and Jay.

'I guess you Marshmallows ain't so bad after all,' I said with a big smile on my face.

'Yeah, and you Eggheads –' began Tim, then he caught himself. 'Sorry, I mean, you Eggingtonians are all right too.'

Everybody burst out laughing. And just like that, our mortal enemies had become our newest friends. Goes to show, there's no point disliking anyone before you get to know 'em properly. Judging someone on where they're from instead of who they are is a great way to make enemies. And, in a world full of killer hamsters, radioactive meteorites and samosa-stealing dads, who needs another enemy? Right?

Oh yeah, and, most importantly of all, if anyone ever gives you the choice of picking hamsters or goldfish, never forget . . .

ALWAYS PICK THE GOLDFISH!!!

I still hate those stupid rats!

DISCOVER THE REST OF THE
BADMAN SERIES . . .

Little Badman and the Invasion of the Killer Aunties

All the teachers have started disappearing from school, and the aunties have taken over! Something very weird is going on. Something alien and slug-like . . .

Little Badman and the Time-travelling Teacher of Doom

When Humza and Umer are sent away to school in Pakistan, it seems like summer is over. But things are about to get wild. Introducing robots, dinosaurs and a whole heap of time travel . . .

Read on for an exclusive preview of

Jaz Santos
vs.
the World

The first book in
The Dream Team
by Priscilla Mante

Coming May 2021

Jaz Santos vs. the World

Things begin to go wrong for Jaz when her
mum moves out, leaving her family behind.
So, determined to fix everything, she creates
her own girls' football team to be the star
her mum always wanted.

First, she recruits a brilliant new group of
friends to join her team. But, after a shaky
start, seven very different personalities to
manage, and no one at school taking the
team seriously, football stardom feels a
long way off . . .

Can Jaz keep everyone – and herself –
out of trouble long enough to convince
her mum to come home?

Dizzy Dancers

Every corner of Bramrock Primary dance studio was buzzing with excited dancers. It was the last class before we got into full rehearsal mode for the annual showcase. This year Ms Morgan's dance club were putting on a jazz-ballet version of *Alice in Wonderland* called *Spinning Alices*. We were going to perform the story of *Alice in Wonderland* through a series of specially choreographed dances.

I scanned the busy dance hall, searching for Charligh. The door swung open and in burst my best friend, looking so relaxed, as if we weren't already exactly seven minutes late for the warm-up. Her long burnt-orange hair was gathered loosely into what could only just pass as a dance-class-approved bun.

'Where have you been?' I said.

She dropped her bag behind the bench and stripped down to her black leotard and pink tights in seconds. A light sprinkling of gold glitter twinkled on the apples of her round, freckled cheeks.

'How about the stage diva sprinkles her glitter dust *after* dance class next time?' I said as we hurried over to join the others at the barre.

Charligh raised her left eyebrow in a perfect arch. 'Since when did Her Royal Lateness care about being on time for anything? You've made us late –' Charligh wiggled her fingers, pretending to tally it up – '444 times this year alone.' Charligh's middle name was Drama. Well, not really, but it should have been. She exaggerated everything, although she was just about right in her calculation of my lateness record.

'Come on, girls! Last ones to get started again?' Ms Morgan swept through the hall, observing everyone's form and ensuring our outfits were just as she wanted.

We took up our positions at the barre. After all, we didn't want to be told more than once by Ms Morgan. She had a special saying about repeating instructions. It was 'twice, not so nice'.

I started my warm-up with a simple mix of pliés and demi-pliés. I looked at Charligh. 'This is our last chance to impress Ms Morgan before she decides on who is playing what in *Spinning Alices*,' I said.

'Either of you'll be lucky to even get in the chorus line,' Rosie Calderwood observed, butting in. 'Everyone knows I'm the best dancer and I'll get the lead role.' She flashed a dimpled smile that didn't reach her ice-blue eyes and smoothed her chocolate-brown hair that was already tucked neatly into a perfect bun.

Now, Ridiculous Rosie is *definitely* not part of my team. In fact, she's kind of a bad guy in this story, so any time she shows up you might want to boo, really loud. Rosie's the leader of the VIPs and, in case you can't tell, she is basically my arch-nemesis.

'Everyone knows Rosie will get the leading role,' Erica Waters gushed like a drippy tap. So Erica is pretty much Rosie's echo. She wasn't too bad until last year, when she was recruited into the VIPs along with Rosie's other sidekick, Summer Singh. Charligh and I call them the Very Irritating People. They had never actually told us what VIP stood for, so we could only assume, based on the evidence . . . I mean, the entire class knew exactly how many times Rosie had been to Orlando, Florida (three times), and just how much spending money she got for her family's annual shopping weekend to Paris (a thousand euros) and how big their villa in Spain was (very big).

Charligh tottered on one leg, stretching the other as high as she could. 'Rosie, do you take extra lessons on the side to become so good – or does it just come naturally to you?'

'Good at what?' Rosie said with her trademark smugness.

'Being incredibly annoying, of course,' Charligh replied.

I snorted.

'You cheeky little –' Rosie hissed.

She was cut short by Ms Morgan's three loud claps – her signal that warm-up was over. We gathered together on the mats in front of her.

'As you all know, this is our last rehearsal before Saturday, when we'll begin on all the group and solo routines for *Spinning Alices*.' She looked round at everyone. 'Consider this a final audition, because I still haven't made my decision on the lead solos. I have an idea, of course, but it's not too late to dazzle me today.'

I grinned at Charligh. I knew it! There was still time to show Ms Morgan that I could be lead soloist at this year's showcase. Mãe (you pronounce it like 'my', by the way, and it's Portuguese for 'mum') bought four tickets last year – one each for her, Dad and my brother Jordan, and the fourth for her youngest sister, my Aunty Bella. Mãe hadn't even made it to any of my parents' evenings for the last two years – Dad was so used to attending by himself now. But there she was at last year's showcase in the front row. It made me feel all sparkly inside when I took the final bow with everyone and heard her cheers above the crowd.

'OK, Dancettes! Split up into your groups of four. It's time for the mirror routine,' Ms Morgan said.

For the mirror routine, each person in the group took a different corner of the room and then performed an identical set of steps so that all four met in the middle. I was in a group with the K triplets from Year 5, so I sat down next to Katy, Keeley and Karina to wait our turn.

This year the showcase was going to be even more special. An army of butterflies took off in my stomach. My mother, who was the best dressmaker in all of Bramrock, was going to make the costumes. Imagine how proud she would be if I turned out to be the girl she had to measure for the grand solo dance at the end? I sat up, back straight, crossing my legs neatly, and noticed a plum-coloured bruise on my ankle. It must have been the vicious tackle Zach Bacon went in for today at lunchtime. *The next time I play him at football*, I thought, *I'll run rings round him*. I'd win the tackle, dribble fast and tight, flick the ball up and head it into the goal. Catching a look at my reflection in the mirrored wall, I realized I looked a bit silly because I'd been miming the actions. I quickly held my head and legs still before anyone saw. Too late.

Rosie waltzed over. 'You're such a weird loser, Jaz. What are you doing – throwing your head about like that? You're an awkward duckling who'll never grow into a graceful swan,' she sneered.

I'd been attending Ms Morgan's after-school dance club twice a week for two years now, learning ballet, jazz and modern dance, but I knew I could be a bit of an elephant among the more dainty dancers. I did goof around sometimes, but even when I tried my hardest, my grands jetés or straddle jumps never seemed to feel as easy to me as dribbling a football down the wing. Still, I wasn't going to let Ridiculous Rosie have the last word.

'Maybe the next time you go on one of your *amazing* holidays, your family can do us all a favour and just leave you there?'

Ms Morgan looked over. 'Jaz! I need you to stop distracting Rosie. We've all worked very hard to get our standards up this term. I won't let you spoil it for everyone.'

The rest of my group were standing in their positions, ready to do the drill. I folded my arms, stung by Ms Morgan's comments. It was dreadfully unfair of her not to notice that Rosie had started it – but then teachers never, ever noticed when Rosie did that sort of thing. Perhaps there was an invisible halo above her smug, heart-shaped face that made everyone treat her like an angel. As I twirled across the studio, I stared hard in the mirror to make sure there weren't invisible horns above my head, because I always got blamed for everything.

This year it *had* to be different. Mãe and Dad had been arguing a lot lately. And even when they weren't actually snapping at each other, there was this horrid feeling in the air that made me feel they were going to start. I had to stop getting into trouble so much because it was just one more thing for them to fight about – like the way they argued over the comments on my report card in Year 5, which were mostly 'must try harder', 'needs to pay more attention' and 'can be a bit disruptive'. So seeing me standing on the stage with a lead part in *Spinning Alices* wouldn't fix everything, but it would help. I could just picture it now: a star-shaped spotlight shining on me, Mãe and Dad crying tears of pride – and Rosie scowling from the shadows . . .

'Ouf!' gasped Katy. She'd collided with me as I began my second pirouette, crashing me out of my dream.

Ms Morgan paused the music. 'OK, let's try that again with the last group. Some of us –' she looked pointedly at me – 'are not paying attention. We need to get this right. How we make our entrance sets the tone for the entire performance. The plan is to make a dramatic entrance, not a comedic one.'

I ignored the snickers of Rosie and Erica from behind me and took a deep breath. *Focus*, I told myself. *Grand jeté. Plié. One, two, three. Pirouette, pirouette, pirou–*

BANG!

This time I skidded all the way past Katy and my elbow connected with the mirrored wall. Then it happened. It always appeared at the worst time. The Laugh was creeping up on me like a rising tidal wave. I tried to keep it down but the pressure was unbearable. It surged in my belly, pulsed up my chest and throat, and chugged out through my mouth and nose.

'Sorry, I'll just –' I spluttered.

Ms Morgan didn't let me finish. 'Take five minutes, Jaz. You can just sit over there and come back when you're ready to stop being silly,' she said. My cheeks burned as I saw a pleased smile flicker across Rosie's face now that I'd given her the chance to steal the spotlight. I watched her land gracefully on her feet after a series of three perfect pirouettes.

It was boring watching the others practise, so I decided to pretend I was actually on the bench, ready to run out on to the pitch to play for England in the finals of the next Women's World Cup. A sports commentator was announcing my arrival on the field . . .

Newly signed Jaz Santos-Campbell runs on to the pitch and immediately gets possession of the ball. She speeds down the centre . . . through three Italian defenders, passes neatly to Rachel Yankey on the wing, who takes it wide before sending it back in a perfect cross to Jaz . . . who SLAMS it in the back of the net with that great left foot in the final minute of play! What a pair of champions! Their supporters have hope again . . . it looks like they could win this . . . Wembley has never seen such a championship final . . .!

The fans were chanting . . . *Jaz! Jaz! She's our star! Jaz! Jaz! . . .*

'Jaz! *Jasmina!*' Ms Morgan said loudly. I leaped to my feet, hoping she hadn't been shouting my name for too long. 'If you'd like to join us from whichever world you've drifted off to, you're more than welcome.'

Luckily we'd moved on from those pesky pirouettes and it was time to practise a new dance. It was a mix of jazz and ballet. Ms Morgan came over to my group, just as it was my turn. I took a deep breath, listening to the music as I moved to the upbeat jazz rhythm, and ended in an arabesque: front leg steady, back leg stretched out, and head tilted upwards. The best way for me to stay perfectly still was to imagine I had my size-five football balancing on my head. I held my breath while Ms Morgan's eyes focused on me.

'Excellent,' she said briskly, before she moved on. I exhaled and relaxed from my position. A seal of approval from Ms Morgan. Finally!

Later, as Charligh and I filed out at the end of class, Ms Morgan stopped me. 'Can I have a word, Jaz?'

'Text me tonight,' Charligh said in a stage whisper. I gave her a small nod as the others zipped out past me.

Perhaps Ms Morgan was feeling bad about how terribly unfair she had been to me earlier. Maybe she was going to apologize because she had finally realized – and not a minute too soon – that it was me, and not Rosie, who had the potential to be a star dancer. My toes tingled. I was already expecting Ms Morgan to give me the biggest hint that she was going to choose *me* as the lead dancer. I giggled, thinking of Rosie's face when I told her . . .

Ms Morgan sighed heavily. 'Jaz, do you still think this is funny?'

I frowned. Judging from the look on her face, maybe I'd got the wrong end of the stick after all and that lead role wasn't quite mine . . . yet.

On your bookmarks, get set, read!

Well hello there! We are

Overjoyed that you have joined our celebration of

Reading books and sharing stories, because we

Love bringing books to you.

Did you know, we are a charity dedicated to celebrating the

Brilliance of reading for pleasure for everyone, everywhere?

Our mission is to help you discover brand new stories and

Open your mind to exciting worlds and characters, from

Kings and queens to wizards and pirates to animals and adventurers and so many more. We couldn't

Do it without all the amazing authors and illustrators, booksellers and bookshops, publishers, schools and libraries out there –

And most importantly, we couldn't do it all without . . .

You!

Changing lives through a love of books and shared reading.

World Book Day is a registered charity funded by publishers and booksellers in the UK & Ireland.

Rob Biddulph

SPONSORED BY

World Book Day — Share a story

From breakfast to bedtime, there's always time to discover and share stories together. You can . . .

1 Take a trip to your local bookshop

Brimming with brilliant books and helpful booksellers to share awesome reading recommendations, you can also enjoy booky events with your favourite authors and illustrators.

Find your local bookshop:
booksellers.org.uk/bookshopsearch

2 Join your local library

That wonderful place where the hugest selection of books you could ever want to read awaits – and you can borrow them for FREE! Plus expert advice and fantastic free family reading events.

Find your local library:
gov.uk/local-library-services/

3 Check out the World Book Day website

Looking for reading tips, advice and inspiration? There is so much to discover at **worldbookday.com**, packed with fun activities, audiobooks, videos, competitions and all the latest book news galore.